TALES FROM THE EDGE
A CHILD'S PLAY STORY COLLECTION

TALES FROM THE EDGE
A CHILD'S PLAY STORY COLLECTION

Cover design by
Paul Tonner

'A Special Delivery' first published in 'A Pocketful of Moondust' by Rebel Books LLP. Re-printed with permission.

About this book

All proceeds from this book are being donated to the Child's Play charity. None of the authors are being paid for their stories and have kindly donated them for inclusion in this book.

Thank you for supporting this charity anthology.

About Childs Play

Since 2003, over 100,000 gamers worldwide have banded together through Child's Play, a community based charity grown and nurtured from the game culture and industry. Over 7 million dollars in donations of toys, games, books and cash for sick kids in children's hospitals across North America, the UK and the rest of the world have been collected since inception.

With over 70 partner hospitals and more arriving every year, you can be sure to find one that needs your help!

When gamers give back, it makes a difference!

You can find out more about the charity from their official website: **www.childsplaycharity.org**

Note

This book contains a number of stories for children of all ages.

The stories are arranged in order by age group, with stories for younger children at the beginning.

Some of the later stories may not be suitable for young children.

Contents

When I'm asleep do my toys wake up?
By Richard Bacon

When I'm asleep do my toys wake up?
I wonder if it's true.
Does my Teddy walk about?
I really wish I knew.

While I dream, the toys can play,
There's no one awake to see.
I don't think anyone knows about them,
No one that is, but me!

Does the rocking horse ride around?
Jumping over books.
Whilst the pirate toys climb about,
Using ropes and hooks.

The toy trains are all chugging,
Around and around the track.
Through the tunnels and stations,
With a clack-ety, clack-ety, clack.

I think my cars may have a race,
The red car and the blue.
Zooming between the building blocks,
And past my wooden Zoo.

The Teddy bears could have a picnic,
I imagine it would be fun.
With sandwiches for all to eat
And for dessert, a sticky bun!

The polar bear and rabbit,
Might dance the night away.
The other toys look on and cheer,
"Well done, that's great, hooray!"

When I wake again next morning,
I take a look around.
Was that dinosaur over there last night?
And that dolly on the ground?

When I'm asleep do my toys wake up?
I wonder if it's true.
Does my Teddy walk about?
I really wish I knew.

I look my Teddy in the eye,
I tell him what I think.
He says nothing, just stares at me,
But I swear I saw him wink…

Chloe and the lost teddy bear
By Richard Bacon

Once upon a time, there was a cow called Chloe.

One day, Chloe, had been playing all over the farm where she lived, having fun with all the other animals, when she heard her mummy calling for her.

"Chloe! It's getting late. Time to get ready for bed!"

Chloe said goodbye to all her friends before running back to the cowshed where she slept with her mummy, but when Chloe looked on her bed, she realised her teddy bear, Fluffy, was missing!

"Oh no!" she sobbed to her mummy. "I can't go to sleep without Fluffy!"

"Oh dear." said her mummy. "Well, let's have a look for Fluffy. I'll look here, while you go and ask the other animals if they have seen him."

Chloe nodded, that was a great idea!

Chloe decided to ask Molly the sheepdog first. Molly was very old and very wise. If anyone could help, Chloe thought it would be Molly!

Molly was lying in her kennel when Chloe arrived and asked, "Please can you help me? I've lost my teddy bear and I don't know where he is. Have you seen a brown teddy bear anywhere on the farm?"

Molly thought for a moment before replying.

"I'm sorry Chloe. I've not seen your teddy bear anywhere."

Chloe felt sad that Molly couldn't help, but then Molly had an idea.

"Why don't you tell me all the things you did today and we'll see if we can find, Fluffy?"

That cheered Chloe up. She closed her eyes and thought about all the things she done that day.

"Well, I was playing with the chickens in the farmyard."

"Come on then!" said Molly getting up. "Let's see if the chickens have seen your teddy bear."

Off they went to see the chickens in their henhouse.

"Hello," said Chloe politely, "Please can you help me? Have you seen a brown teddy bear anywhere on the farm?"

The chickens clucked for a moment before one of them answered Chloe. "Cluck, Cluck! Sorry, Chloe. We haven't seen any teddy bears. "

Chloe was disappointed.

"Where else have you been today?" asked Molly.

Chloe thought again for a moment. "I was playing with the pigs as well."

So off went Chloe and Molly to see the pigs in the pig sty.

"Hello, have you seen a brown teddy bear anywhere on the farm?" Chloe asked the pigs.

The pigs oinked to one another for a moment before one of them answered Chloe. "Oink, Oink! Sorry, Chloe. We haven't seen any teddy bears."

Chloe moo-ed sadly. Where could her teddy bear be?

"Have you been anywhere else today?" asked Molly.

Again Chloe closed her eyes and tried to remember what she had done. "I went to see the horses!" she said.

The horses all lived together in the stable. Chloe went over with Molly to speak to them.

"Hello, have you seen a brown teddy bear anywhere on the farm?"

The horses neighed to one another for a moment before one of them answered Chloe. "Neigh, Neigh! Sorry, Chloe. We haven't seen any teddy bears."

Chloe was starting to feel very sad. No one had seen her missing teddy bear and she began to wonder if she would ever see him again.

Bravely she closed her eyes to remember anywhere else she had been. "I was in the field with all the sheep." She told Molly.

So Chloe and Molly trotted off to the field where all the sheep lived. Chloe really hoped they could help her.

"Hello, have you seen a brown teddy bear anywhere on the farm?" she asked the sheep.

The sheep baa-ed to one another for a moment before one of them answered Chloe. "Baaa! Sorry, Chloe. We haven't seen any teddy bears."

Now Chloe was really sad. She began to feel tears building up in her eyes. But just then, Tilly, one of the lambs Chloe had played with earlier, came to speak to her.

"We did have a picnic under the old oak tree… and we all had our teddy bears with us then. Perhaps he's still there?"

"Oh, thank you Tilly! I remember now!" Chloe turned to Molly. "Let's go see if he's still there."

Chloe felt very hopeful as she and Molly went across the field to the old oak tree.

Sure enough when they got there, they found Fluffy, still sat by the tree!

"There you are, Fluffy!" said Chloe happily.

Molly smiled, "You'd better get back to your mummy. It's starting to get late."

Molly nodded and ran happily back to the cow shed, holding Fluffy very tightly.

Chloe's mummy smiled as Chloe lay down for bed.

"I'll never lose you again, Fluffy!" said Chloe, before yawning and falling fast asleep.

Goodnight Chloe!

The Princess and the Gardener
By Beth Bowler

Once upon a time,
In a land not so far away.

A tiny Princess cried,
Where the tiny Princess lay.

Her heart it was not broken,
The Princess was not sad.

She was full of blinding rage,
At the folk who made her mad.

Her land was under threat,
The homes of all the Small.

By the constant selfish actions of the folk they named

'The Tall'.

Tall wandered through the land,
Over all the tiny places.

They did not see the fear,
On the tiny bright red faces.

Never looking down,
Never hearing cries!

When would the Tall folk see?
When would they realise?

The princess had decided,
To seek some counsel from the moon.

So she ordered the tallest tower to be built...

And very soon...

The tower was complete!

The Princess, cross, but still quite fair,
Began her long and daunting journey...
Up the steep and spiral stairs.

When finally, she reached the top,
She fell on desperate knees. Lost for sense and words she
heard herself cry...

'Help me please!'

Surprisingly she heard...

'OMG!'

'A tiny little lady, crying tiny little tears,
With a tiny furrowed brow, hiding tiny fairy fears.'

Looking directly at the man, the princess began to say,

*'My people are not yours you fool, to mock and scare and
slay!'*

'I'm not sure what you're saying,
I'm the gardener not a fool!
I know not of your problem Miss,
But it doesn't sound that cool.'

She took a deep big breath, looked right into his eyes...
She stated very clearly, so the man would realise...

'It's you, you big old bully, you're killing all our spirits.'
Our land you've worn away, you know not your strength nor
know your limits.'

The gardener pulled a face,
He held his head into his hands.

'I thought fairies were all nonsense,
I don't believe in fairylands.'

'But here is this tiny lady, crying tiny little tears.
With a tiny furrowed brow, hiding tiny fairy fears.'

The princess saw a tear fall from his big green eyes.
She had not thought about it, maybe he did not realise.

They discussed a resolution.
The gardener gave up a bit of land.

The tiny princess smiled again and stepped on to his
enormous hand.

And so in the gardener's garden, you may now understand,

Grows a tiny patch of wilderness,

Well that is quite on purpose…

To protect the fairy land.

Who wants to be a tortoise?
By Richard Bacon

Todd the tortoise didn't want to be a tortoise anymore.

Todd and his friends were hungry, so they had decided to go to the fruit trees at the edge of the jungle where they lived.

All the animals rushed off to get the fruit trees, but Todd was a tortoise, and tortoises are not very fast creatures.

Todd watched Harry and Luca, the monkeys, swing through the trees, moving very quickly through the Jungle.

"I wish I was a monkey, swinging through the trees." Thought Todd.

Penny the Parrot flew quickly between the trees, her bright red feathers shining in the sun.

"I wish I was parrot, flying through the air with bright colourful feathers." Thought Todd.

Marty the Cheetah ran and jumped quickly across the ground.

"I wish I was a cheetah, they can run really fast". Thought Todd.

He ambled along after the other animals, wishing he could be different.

As he walked along, it started to rain, a few drops at first, then more and more and more.

Todd pulled his head into his shell and waited for the rain to stop.

Inside his shell he was warm and dry; he listened to the rain pitter-patter on top of his shell.

The rain didn't last very long, and soon the sun was shining again.

Todd poked his head out from his shell and looked around. Just ahead he could see his friends huddled together under a tree. They all looked very wet from the rain.

"Why are you still dry?" Asked Harry and Luca together.

"I went into my shell until the rain finished." Said Todd.

"I wish I had a shell like a tortoise." Said Harry, Luca nodded in agreement.

Todd thought about that and smiled, it was nice to have a shell sometimes.

The animals shook off the rain and began rushing towards the fruit trees again.

Todd sighed and plodded on as fast as he could go.

A few minutes later Todd came to a slight bump in the ground, he climbed to the top and quickly stopped as he saw a big, muddy puddle just below. Marty the Cheetah was sitting in the middle of the puddle, his fur all wet and covered in mud!

"I was going too fast". Said Marty sadly, "I couldn't stop in time like you. I wish I was as careful as a tortoise".

Todd thought about that and smiled, sometimes it was useful not being too fast.

Marty shook off the mud and they set off again towards the fruit trees.

By now they were nearly at the edge of the jungle, and so just a short while later they reached the fruit trees, and together the friends all ate the delicious, juicy fruit.

After they had finished, the friends decided to play a game.

"Let's play hide and seek!" Said Marty. "I'll go first. You all hide and I'll try and find you."

Marty started counting, "1, 2, 3, 4, 5..."

The animals all went and hid. Todd walked over to some rocks and tucked his head into his shell.

"...6, 7, 8, 9, 10, coming ready or not!" Marty cried.

Marty immediately looked up into the trees and spotted Harry and Luca.

"You always hide in the trees!" Marty laughed. He looked around again for Penny the parrot and Todd.

"I can see you behind that bush Penny," said Marty,

"Your bright red feathers give you away."

Penny came out from behind the bush. Marty and the others all looked around for Todd, but they just couldn't see him.

"We give up!" Laughed Marty, "Todd, you win!"

Todd popped his head out and walked away from the rocks.

"There you are", said Penny, "You looked just a like a rock. I wish I was like a tortoise so I could win at hide and seek."

Todd thought about that and smiled, sometimes it was useful not being bright and colourful.

As all the friends made their way home slowly together, Todd thought that perhaps being a tortoise was not so bad after all!

The Moonlight Express
By Richard Bacon

"All aboard!" the conductor cries
The Moonlight Express is here!
The train to take us to the land of Nod,
It runs throughout the year.

When you're tired and sleepy,
There's one thing you should know.
Just climb aboard this magic train,
And off to sleep we go!

Gleaming in the moonlight,
The paint all bright and red.
Just use your imagination,
Whilst tucked up in your bed.

The wheels go round, we're on our way,
You're welcome one and all!
When it's time to dream, this train is here,
For everyone, large and small.

The engine puffs as it steams along,
It's headlight shining strong.
Lighting up the way ahead,
As we speed along.

Close your eyes and lay down your head,
We're off on our magic ride.
Make sure your pillow is nice and soft,
And on the train we'll glide.

Clack-ety clack through Dreamy Fields,
The stars all twinkle brightly.
And past the village of Snugglesville,
Hug your teddy tightly.

'Gently now, gently now',
The rails seem to say.
'Softly now, softly now',
As we continue on our way.

Through the tunnel and up the hill,
Along the tracks we steam.
So rest your head, drift off to sleep,
It's nearly time to dream.

The sounds now start to fade away,
Our bed so soft and warm.
Into the land of Nod go we,
Until the light of dawn.

As so we sleep through the night,
Safe and sound once more.
Till the 'morrow, when once again,
The Moonlight Express we'll board.

Goodnight everyone!

Chloe and the little alien
By Richard Bacon

Once upon a time, there was a cow called Chloe.
One night, Chloe the cow just could not get to sleep.
All over the farm where she lived, all the other animals were
sleeping soundly. But Chloe just could not get to sleep.

She went over to the next field to count the sheep, but
that didn't work either.

Chloe did not know what to do. She stared up at the
twinkling stars in the dark night sky and wondered if she
would ever fall to sleep!

But as Chloe looked at the stars she noticed one of
them seemed to be getting brighter and brighter, and larger
and larger!

Chloe stared in wonder as the light came towards her,
then, stopped just above her field.

It was then that Chloe realised it was a spaceship! As
she watched, three legs popped out the bottom of the
spaceship and it landed in the field. Then a door opened in
the spaceship, and with a bright light behind him, out stepped
a little green alien.

The alien was wearing a bright blue spacesuit over his
green skin, with silver space boots. Chloe noticed he had four
fingers, but most unusually of all, the little alien had small
stalks on the top of his head, on which were his eyes!

The little alien held out his hand to Chloe. "Hello, my
name is Zeebit. Please do not be afraid."

"Hello," she replied, "my name is Chloe. Nice to meet
you."
She frowned. "Why would I be afraid?"

The alien sighed. "Every time I try and say hello to
someone new they run away. Just because I look different."

Chloe shook her head. "That's silly! I'm different to
the chickens, but I'm not scared of them. There's no need to
be scared just because someone is a little different."

Zeebit blinked his eyes. "You are a very wise cow, Chloe."

He gestured to his spaceship. "Would you like to go for a ride?"

"Oh, yes please!" said Chloe.

Chloe went with Zeebit in his spaceship, they flew high over Chloe's farm, and then higher and higher into the night sky.

Zeebit told Chloe all about his home planet, and Chloe told Zeebit all about the farm she lived on, and all the animals that lived there with Chloe.

As Zeebit flew around the moon, Chloe looked out the window and asked, "Is the moon really made of green cheese?"

Zeebit shrugged. "I don't know. Let's land and find out!"

They quickly landed and got out of the spaceship. Chloe sniffed the surface of the moon. "Hmmm, this doesn't smell like the cheese back on the farm."

Zeebit started laughing and shouting to Chloe. "Look at me!" Chloe looked round to see Zeebit as he jumped and flew high into the air. Chloe tried it too and also flew high into the sky. Much higher than when she was back home.

Both Chloe and Zeebit laughed loudly as they played together on the moon, leaping high into the sky.

As they played, Chloe suddenly yawned.

"Oh, sorry," she said. "I was having trouble sleeping, but now I feel really tired."

"Don't worry," said Zeebit, "I'll take you back home now so you can go to sleep."

The two friends climbed back about Zeebit's spaceship, and very soon they were back again in Chloe's field.

Chloe yawned again and spoke sleepily to Zeebit. "Thank you for a wonderful night. Will I see you again?"

Zeebit thought for a moment. "Well I live very far

away so it might not be for a while." He smiled and pointed to a twinkling star in the sky. "But if ever you can't sleep, just look up and remember me and our adventure, and I'm sure you'll soon drop off to sleep."

Chloe smiled. "Thank you. I will miss you. Goodbye Zeebit."

"Goodbye Chloe." Said Zeebit, as he stepped back into his spaceship.

Chloe watched as Zeebit flew high into the sky and off, into the night.

Just a few moments later Chloe was fast asleep, dreaming about adventures with Zeebit, far away in space.

Goodnight Chloe!

The Lie (A True Story)
By Chris Preece

It's playtime. We all run about having fun.
We're pretending we all have to rescue my Mum,
She's been shot at the station by a terrible spy,
A very small start to a very big lie.

Whistle blows, and we all line up to go in.
Still excited, I'm chatting, my face a big grin,
"You boy, be quiet, why are you talking?"
"My Mum's been shot, she's barely still walking."

She stops, her face changes, her voice goes quite small,
"You poor little thing, I'd no clue at all."
I hadn't meant this to happen, but I won't burst her bubble,
I'd rather she worried, than I was in trouble.

So that's how it starts, soon everyone knows,
About my poor mother's fictional woes.
The story gets bigger, I suppose it's an honour,
"Just that little bit higher, and she'd be a goner."

Everyone knows, with one big exception,
My mother hears nothing of my great deception.
Until comes the day of the school sponsored walk.
And she finds herself subject of neighbourhood talk.

They start shaking her hand, and they tell her she's brave.
By the time that she finds me, my predicament's grave.
And so I discovered to my cost that day,
Lies come back to find you, they don't go away.

And still, even now, to my irritation,
People ask me, "Was your Mum shot at the station?"
I look at them straight in the eye so they know
I'm telling the truth when I say to them – 'No'.

A Special Delivery
By Richard Bacon

"Splattering Dragons spit!"

Henry pulled his flying carpet sharply to the right, just in time, as a glowing, sizzling green orb flashed by where he had been just a moment earlier.

"These guys mean business!" Said Henry.

Checking the skies ahead he risked a look back over his shoulder, sure enough the black unmarked flying carpet was still there behind him, it's cabin windows were tinted black, but he could see one of the occupants as he leaned out the side window, pointing a glowing green wand in Henry's direction.

As he frantically searched the skyways ahead for a turn off, he shook his head.   This is not what he had expected when he'd become a Trainee Postman, 2nd class.

It had all started a few hours before, not long after Henry had completed his usual delivery run around the academic district of Enchantia City.

Henry's delivery route wasn't the most glamorous run in the postal service; it mainly involved carrying large tomes of magic books to the various schools for Witches, Wizards and Woglies. Woglies being small, fur covered elf like magic creatures, just in case you didn't know.

Though quite tiring, it was not considered dangerous, although there had been that one time when one of the books on monsters had tried to eat him, but that was a rare exception.

As usual, after completing all the deliveries, Henry had returned to sorting office number 12 in his standard issue, red coloured Royal Postal Company flying carpet, and reported to his boss, an unusually tall dwarf named Edmund. And as usual, Edmund seemed to be in a bad mood.

"HENRY!" He shouted, spotting Henry as soon as he

entered the office.

Henry trudged into Edmunds office, wondering why he had been summoned.

Without even a 'Hello', Edmund started talking. "All my workers are busy, or caught up in that Ogre Festival mess over on the other side of the city"

The annual Ogrefest caused a lot of disruption within the city, not to mention the bad smells, no really, please don't mention them, but the Ogres were big spenders, so the city's merchants were at least somewhat happy to have them, as long as they weren't involved in the cleanup afterwards anyway.

Edmund continued. "So, I have this special delivery I need you to make. It's for a Grand Master Fimbleberry, he's waiting for it and it's very important, so don't mess it up!"

Edmund picked up an innocent looking small rectangular parcel wrapped in brown paper, tied up with some white string, and passed it over to Henry.

"Right, off you go, watch out for traffic, and remember to get a signature." Edmund waved his arms as a signal for Henry to leave the office.

Henry took the package and put it carefully into his post bag. A Grand Master! The name was only given to very powerful sorcerers, the package could be anything, and Edmund had said it was very important; it was almost certainly something magical Henry thought.

Henry headed out the sorting office and down the stone steps leading out towards the flying carpet park, but just as he was leaving, a voice came from the shadows by the doorway.

"Pssst, hey you human, wait a minute."

Henry stopped and turned towards the voice.

From out of the shadows stepped a small goblin, dressed in a dark green outfit with a matching green, tall pointy hat on his head.

Now Henry tried not to judge people before he knew

them, but goblins are generally known not to be too trustworthy, so he pulled his bag a little closer to his side and kept a firm grip on the opening.

"Yes, how can I help you?" He asked in his most polite voice, after all the goblin could well be a customer.

The goblin hopped from foot to foot as he spoke to Henry. "You don't have a package for Grand Master Fimbleberry do you? Only he sent me to collect it."

Henry thought quickly, he was supposed to deliver special packages personally; it was unusual for anyone to come and collect a package without calling ahead first. Plus he wasn't sure he could trust the goblin. Now normally Henry always told the truth, but in this case he felt it might be better to be cautious. So instead he shook his head.

"Sorry sir, I don't. Perhaps you should ask at the reception desk?" He added helpfully.

The goblin shook his head quickly, "No, no, that's fine." His eyes squinted as he looked closely at Henry. "Are you sure? It's very important that the Grand Master gets the package as soon as possible." He said.

"Oh yes sir. Now I must be on my way. Good day."

Henry walked as quickly as he could to his carpet, hovering in the staff parking bays. Quickly he got into the cabin attached to the carpet and pulled on the controls to take off and head into the skyways around the city.

He looked out the cabins window; the goblin was speaking to a large man and pointing at Henry's carpet.

Luckily as it was not rush hour, the skyways were fairly clear and Henry was able to get into lane and head off across the city towards the address on the mysterious package. He shook off his thoughts over the goblin, after all he was going to deliver the package, and so even if the goblin had indeed been sent by the Grand Master, the package would soon be delivered anyway.

It was just a short while later when he noticed that a dark black carpet behind him had been taking the same turns as he had for the last few minutes.

He glazed anxiously into the mirror to watch the black carpet behind. And it was then he saw another black carpet appear behind the first one. Now there were two of them!

Henry's heart began to beat a little bit faster, were they following him, or was he just being silly?

At the next turn he decided to change at the last moment to see what the two carpets behind him did. He approached the next corner as if he was going to turn left and looked back, the carpets behind were also in the lane for turning left. As he reached the corner he suddenly turned to the right instead, causing a witch on a broomstick to quickly move out of the way.

Henry looked back as he shouted, "Sorry", out of his window.

The witch was shaking a wrinkled arm at him and shouting some quite rude things as well. Then from around the corner the two black carpets appeared, also turning right, almost knocking the witch off her broom!

Henry's heart was definitely beating faster now as he watched the carpets behind.

One of the carpets sped up and moved beside Henry's. As the window rolled down, a large man wearing black sunglasses looked over to Henry.

"Land the carpet kid, we don't want to harm you. We just want the package."

Henry did not like being called a kid, and so despite the fear growing in his stomach he felt a tinge of anger. Besides, these guys didn't seem friendly, so he didn't think it would be a good idea to give them package anyway.

He looked ahead, where was a police warlock when you needed one?

A glowing sign rushed by as they continued to speed along the skyway between the tall buildings in this part of the city.

This gave Henry an idea, and at the next turning he

quickly turned right.

The carpet next to him did not make the turn and carried on, but the one behind made the turn and continued following.

Henry looked back to see where they were, just in time to see a glowing wand appear out of the window of the carpet and a bright green glow appear before zooming straight towards him.

"Splattering Dragons spit" Cried Henry, oh yes, sorry, this is where you joined the story isn't it?

Henry kept looking for the turn off he was waiting for, all the while keeping an eye on the pursuing carpet behind him.

Just ahead he saw the glowing sign he'd been expecting, and with a sly smile he prepared for the turn ahead.

"Let's see if you guys are ready for this!" He announced to his pursuers.

Quickly he took the next turn to the left, he then pulled the carpets controls, bringing the carpet to a stop, before dropping down almost to the ground. He looked up to watch as the black carpet rushed round the corner, and as he had hoped, ran straight into Melvin the Magnificent's Deluxe Dragon Wash!

So intent were they on following Henry, his pursuers had failed to notice the glowing signs indicating the directions to the dragon wash.

Luckily for them there wasn't a dragon in the wash at the moment, but their entry had trigged the wash, and the cabin of the black carpet was now filled with soapy bubbles, whilst sprays of water washed over the carpet.

As the occupants leaned out of the window, spluttering bubbles, Henry waved a cheeky salute and set off again towards Grand Masters Fimbleberry's address to deliver the package.

Henry had just gotten his breathing under control when another glowing orb flashed by his carpet and shattered into bright green sparks on the wall of the building by his side.

He looked about in horror, the second black carpet was back!

Even from the distance separating them, Henry could see the anger on the face of the man lining up his wand at Henry.

"Not again!" He cried as he accelerated his carpet.

Another green glow whizzed by.

"Wizards warts, that one was close!" Henry's mind raced, how could he lose the carpet and complete his delivery?

In the distance ahead he noticed green and red smoke rising into the air, Ogrefest!

Henry dodged yet another glowing blast from behind, his luck had to be running low, at any moment one of the glowing green orbs would hit him, and who knows what would happen then?

Ogrefest was held in the Enchanted Park located in the heart of Enchantia City. As Henry dived past other carpets on the skyway and headed straight for the Ogrefest, he began scanning the park ahead, looking for some way to lose the carpet giving chase.

Below were spread out hundreds of tents, large and small, along with the various activities and attractions for the ogres.

He could make out the rotten log throwing contest, as well as the slug eating contest, uggh!

And there ahead was the High Dive into the Stinky Swamp Competition. Henry could see the ogres eagerly queuing just behind the diving board, waiting to jump into the bubbling, smelly swamp below.

He watched the ogres jump one by one, and a crazy idea came to his head. 'Maybe, just maybe' his mind thought.

Trying to keep one eye on the carpet behind he flew down over the ogres below and headed straight for the diving area.

Henry closed his eyes his carpet flew under the diving board, just as an ogre began his jump.

Henry shot by as the ogre hung momentarily in the air, then as he started falling, the black carpet followed Henry's path.

BAAaaammm!

The ogre landed on the roof of the black carpet, with a bang before his weight pushed the carpet down, down until… Splat!

The flying carpet and ogre splattered into the swamp as one.

Henry threw up an arm in victory, it had worked! He circled around to take a closer look.

Below the occupants of the black carpet were clambering out of the cabin and into the swamp. Around them were several angry ogres, pretty normal for an ogre really, but in this case they were really angry!

Henry winced in sympathy for a moment at their plight, but quickly turned back on course to deliver the package that had surely caused all this chaos and trouble in the first case.

"I'll be glad to get rid of you." He said to the package within his bag.

Without further incident, Henry soon located the address of Grand Master Fimbleberry, parked his carpet and approached the door. With a cautious look around, he rang the doorbell.

"Just a moment!"

The door creaked open to reveal an old man with a long flowing beard and sparkly eyes.

"Come in, come in, I've been expecting you." Said Grand Master Fimbleberry..

"Your package, sir." Said Henry whilst pulling the package from his bag. "I expect it's very important?" He enquired curiously.

"Oh yes".

"And magical?" Henry probed.

"Some might say that indeed." Replied the Grand Master. He leaned closer to Henry and said in a low voice. "You may think I'm silly, but I was even worried someone may try and intercept it whilst it was in the post!"

Henry nodded, "Well actually…" He began, but the Grand Master continued.

"Oh yes, I know old Filius Burplebum of Burplebum Sweets would love to get his hands on this."

"Really!" Exclaimed Henry before he considered the words. "Wait, sweets?"

"Indeed, he's been after my Aunt Copperpot's fudge recipe for years. If he'd know you'd got it he'd probably have sent someone to turn you into a toad or something in order to get it!"

The Grand Master opened the package and removed a folded parchment upon which a fudge recipe was written. Below were several pieces of fudge.

The Grand master passed one of the pieces to Henry.

"Here you go, have a taste."

"Fudge?" Was all Henry could manage to say.

The Grand Master signed the form Henry had provided and handed it back to the dumbstruck trainee postman,

"Well good day, thank you again."

As Henry left without another word, and the door closed behind him, he could only stare at the piece of fudge in his hand.

He'd been through all that for a fudge recipe?

Stunned, he put the fudge in his mouth without thinking and began wearily making his way back to his parked carpet.

"Witches whiskers!" Exclaimed Henry.

It was indeed the most amazing, fantastic, tasty, wonderful, magical fudge he'd ever tasted!

The Visit
By Chris Lill

"I love coffee as much as the next person but any more and I'll be up and down all night like a bleeding Jack-in-a-box" she said.

"What about a smoothie luv?" he said.

"Nah. Can't we just leave now? It's been an hour at least'" she said

"You heard what the TV told us. I'm not risking it. It's warm in here anyway and I'm not charging for the food and drink. Have as much as you want; the food will be only be chucked out at the end of the day anyway. Normally catch them tramps rifling through the bins at closing time." He said.

"No chance of them scrambling through the bins at the moment. They'd be absolutely mental to be outside during The Visit. 'spose if they're drunk then they might be out there but you'd like to think that some kind soul might take them in until it passes." She said.

"Are people that nice? Seems to be that everyone's just out for themselves these days. Horror films have taught me never to take a strange person in, might be an axe murderer. No good can come from it. Seems like the rich just keep on getting richer and the rest of us just fight over a few decent jobs. People need to be more selfless, far too selfish. Not right. Really not." He said.

"But what does all that money matter when there is no protection from it. No-one's ever spoken about The Visit and the one's that have witnessed it refuse to say what they actually saw. Just seem to have that smug smile as if they know something that we don't. Like they doubt the Government warnings of the dangers that The Visit brings." She said.

Immediately, the ground tremored and the windows rattled in their frames. Not forceful enough for their mugs to leave the table but enough for the shop's sign to swing violently and slam against the front door. She was only able to see the tops of the window frame shudder as the piled up tables and impromptu pyramid of chairs obscured all but the top foot of glass. Darkness slipped in through this upper part of the window. The forced obscurity of the outside world unsettled her as it had done when she went camping in the abundant darkness of the Highlands. Yet, electricity still worked, as it always did and they had enough food and drink for a good few weeks. The longest she knew that The Visit had ever run for was for 14 hours. She couldn't go that long without talking to her friends or gawking on the internet. What were they supposed to do for keeping clean? Even camping holidays offered more than a rudimentary basin to wash with. Plus they were those annoying pressurised taps.

The door creaked.

"Oh my god, oh my god, oh my god' she said panic-stricken.

"Don't worry, it's probably the wind. You know how it gets stronger the closer it gets. Always windier this time of year."

"How can you be so sure? Can't we shift those fridges over to the door? We don't need all of them?" She pleaded.

"I don't reckon my back could withstand shifting one of them acapella. No offence luv, but you don't look like you'd be able to help me move one of them. Look, I've never done more than we have for protection. Anyway, if it's our time for The Visit, no amount of fridges are going to help. They can hinder, but can't stop."

"Why doesn't my mobile work? It's absurd. We can heat food and cool the stuff, yet I can't call someone."

"Something to do with static electricity. Heard someone go on about it once. Can't say I understood or really paid much attention. It's to be expected though I guess."

He continued. "What are you gonna say anyway? 'Hi mum, I'm stuck. Can't do much. Hope we don't get The Visit. Fingers crossed.' Should have taken the government advice and kept some work with you in your bag or a decent book. Even write a book. Everyone's got one in them apparently. Can't think I've got much to say in all honesty."

The door creaked again. This time more forcefully and unnaturally. It was no wind pressuring the entrance. In her rush to run behind the counter she managed to knock over the large number of shopping bags she had accumulated whilst bunking truanting that afternoon.

"Oi, you can't go behind there, employees only."

"Whatever. Do I look like I care? Who's gonna tell me off? That? I'm getting in the fridge."

An audible click as the plug was pulled out of its socket. He looked on as she deposited cartons of milk - both soya and bovine – firmly on the floor.

"It's freezing." She uttered blatantly with her arms submerged in the chest fridge.

"What did you expect? It's not a sunbed. Wouldn't catch me getting in that. Foolish if you ask me."

The door creaked again, snow blew in and he made a run for the small walk-in fridge near to the toilets. She realised that there was just about enough space for the two of them, but it was a squeeze and meant she would have to endure his slight sweaty aroma. He was equally unimpressed with having to tolerate her sickly sweet perfume. She squeezed in with him.

"Close the door" He said.

"No. How will we breathe? Won't we run out of oxygen? I don't want to suffocate to death."

"Look, if it gets difficult to breathe, the handle allows us to open the fridge from the inside. This is bloody stupid though, why are we getting into a fridge anyway? The chance of it coming here…"

The door creaked again. This time the chairs at the peak of the pyramid toppled down taking a few lower down ones with them. The pyramid disintegrated and the exposed window area became considerably larger. This event was

33

followed by a large smash and the door rattled in its frame. So much so that the door appeared to be coming away from its hinges. They slammed the fridge closed. Panic had taken up residence in their eyes. She tried to speak but he mouthed an urgent 'shhhhh' at her. Their enclosed asylum kept out much of the shop's noise but they could hear the door open violently. A smash of glass was followed by the crunch of many feet on the shattered shards. How many creatures were there? The amount of crunching glass suggested a great deal. A tear rolled down her cheek.

It was clear that whatever was in the shop was not trying to hide its presence and had little fear of discovery. From inside the fridge the sound suggested the visitor was larger than the two of them together and it appeared to have difficulty navigating the shop floor without clattering into tables and chairs. He began to reach into his jacket pocket, which was proving difficult due to the confined space. "What you doing?" she whispered through gritted teeth; her anger was etched all over her face. "I'm gonna video it, no-one's got that on camera. It'll make us a fortune."

"Are you mad?" she hissed. "You're not going out there. God only knows what will happen to you."

"Course not. I'm just gonna pop the door ajar and poke the camera out."

"But once the door's open, it could get in here easily. Don't you dare."

It was clear he was going to ignore her pleading; that much was evident from his continued pocket probing. A few seconds later and the camera was in his left hand. He turned it on. The camera automatically lit up to compensate for the darkness of the fridge. He changed the settings in order to turn the light off, aware that this might attract the thing's attention when the camera was posited outside the fridge. His arm moved to open the fridge but she held it back. He wrestled his arm away from her and popped the fridge door open with the internal handle.

The sound of the shop hit them both. The sound of silence. There was no crunching glass, or clattering furniture to signal its movement. There was an eerie and suspicious calm beyond the fridge's door. With camera firmly in hand, he manoeuvred it round so that the lens made a slow sweep of the room. He had no way of knowing what was out there as the door was only slightly open. He could only see part of the basin next to the fridge and a slim slither of window in front of it, the rest of the room was obscured from his vision. After 30 long seconds he pulled his hand back and closed the fridge door as quietly as he could. He rewound the footage. The fridge seemed noticeably colder with the door shut and more than ever he wished that they could just get out of there. Both of them studied the camera screen as the footage began to play. The clip was never going to be worth any money, showing 30 seconds of an exceedingly messy coffee shop. The goods and gifts she'd purchased were spread all over the floor. A mixture of relief and disappointment came over them.

It had gone.

They remained silent until he made moves to open the door to give his mobile another risky excursion. The process was repeated again and with exactly the same results.

"Let's go back out there, it's gone." He suggested.

Shivering, she agreed. Whatever it was, it had gone. That much the camera had shown them. They pushed the door open.

The café was how they had left it. Messy. They crouched down to check under the tables and checked the shop for evidence of what The Visit was about. There was nothing different.

Apart from an old man who walked out of the toilet. They instantly recognised Him.

He was exactly how they'd always thought He would look.

He had the grey beard that had historically been attributed to Him by artists and stories of old.

His face radiated knowledge and kindness.

So, the unbelievers were wrong, He was real. Neither of them had been believers for many years. In a world of science and the need for proof they never considered He really could exist.

Billions of people who had had the faith to believe in His existence were right. This was no figment of the imagination for the weak-minded.

Whilst his believers had been ridiculed and criticised for believing in Him, here in front of a coffee shop worker and a truanting pupil was the proof of this embodiment of goodness.

Although the immediate shock of His appearance had taken the pair of them aback, they were both now furiously trying to figure out whether they had acted morally, kindly and selflessly or was He here to judge their previous actions negatively.

It was the shared understanding that now was the time of their judgement that brought both of them to their knees in front of Him.

Calmness washed over them as they awaited the verdict from this supernatural being of miracles.

He cleared his throat.

"I must apologise for startling you in this way. Sometimes Rudolph and the others get the wrong entrance…."

A Werewolf Ate My Homework
By Richard Bacon

Wednesday afternoon math class. It's never going to be the highlight of your life, not even the day, so you'll forgive me if I'm sitting here just daydreaming. It's not even that I dislike maths, and without sounding big headed I already know everything Mr Philkins is trying to teach us anyway.

Perhaps I should explain.

My name is Valeros, and I'm a faerie.
Now before I go on, let's clear up a few misconceptions. I am not six inches high with wings. Faeries are actually human size, usually a little taller than human average actually, we're slender built with pale skin. We're not immortal, we live for hundreds of years, but we can still be killed like you. Generally speaking we're not particularly stronger than humans, but we are quicker, more nimble, and yes we can perform magic.

Also I know there are stories about faeries as tricksters and practical jokers, well, ok, I'll admit some faeries do play tricks on humans, but hey, who's perfect? You humans sure aren't angels either.

We live both in your world, and our own realm, I know you humans like your scientific explanations, so I guess you'd call it a parallel universe or something. Someone tried to explain it all to me once, but I forget the whole deal. It just exists ok? And before you ask, No, I don't know anything about the tooth fairy!

So what do faeries do? Well generally we help keep nature going, you think those seasons just change by themselves? Rain and snow just happens? Well let me tell you something, without us things would soon start going wrong, really wrong.

But what exactly is it that I do, I hear you ask? Well you know how Vampires, Werewolves, Gorrmons and such like only exist in movies and books? Well you keep thinking that, it'll help you sleep a little better. My clan's job is to make sure none of these 'imaginary' creatures harms a human. I'm your bodyguard if you will. Although don't get too sentimental, sure I quite like humans, but our main task is to ensure you don't learn of the magical world, to do so would endanger our realm. A very curious lot are humans I've found.

It's for this reason that I live in your world, go to school, learn how you…

"VAL SMITH! Are you paying attention?"

That's me, I use the name Val in your world, and I know Smith isn't original, but we can't have humans knowing our true names can we, do you know what power that would give you?

Mr Philkins looks mad so I'd better answer him. "Uh, yes Sir, sorry Sir."

Mr Philkins still looks mad.

"Well then, I look forward to seeing your homework tomorrow; I'll give it special attention."

Damn. We're not supposed to draw too much attention to ourselves, this means I'd better make sure that my homework is good. Mind you it should be, as I was explaining earlier I think I know everything Mr Philkins is trying to teach me. Funny thing is I'm probably nearly double his age. I'm ninety five; this will be the fourth time I've graduated from school. Told you, really long lives. I'll look like a human teenager for about another forty or so years. The aging process will slow down once I get past one hundred and fifty, then I'll be my human twenties for a couple of centuries.

The bell goes sparing me from further attention; I pack

up my things to go.

"Hey, you wanna meet up tonight?"

That's Kyle Redfield, my friend. Yes, he's human, and no, he doesn't know about me.

"Henry's parents are away so we're setting up a four system linkup and playing all night!" Continues Kyle.

Kyle loves videogames, and thanks to my reflexes I'm pretty good at them too, so that's our main thing. He's perhaps not the most exciting human around, but he doesn't stand out and we have a good time together.

"I'll try. I'd better head for the library first and get this homework done else Mr P is gonna kill me."

Kyle nods. "Ok, well you know where we'll be, I'll be heading there later myself, hope to see you there."

Kyle heads off as I turn towards the library.

It takes over an hour to do my homework; I want to make sure it's good, although not perfect.

It's about then that my phone goes off; I've got a text message. Sure we use mobile's, your technical magic is pretty handy sometimes, so why not?

FROM: LEONAS
PATROL TONIGHT, WARNING FROM FAYE,
WEREWOLVES. MEET NOW.

Leonas is our elder, he's in charge. Leonas looks old, which for a faerie means he's really old! Some reckon he's over two thousand years old. He won't tell anyone how old he really is.

Faye is actually half human, half faerie, an interesting combination to be sure, and a story for another time. What's important is that Faye has been gifted with foresight; she can see glimpses of the future. She helps guide us to possible trouble... then it's up to us to stop it.

I finish up my work and head out, Faye's house is about a mile and half away from my school. It won't take me long to get there.

I'm the last to arrive, the others of my group are already here. We hunt as a trio.

"You're late."

That's Tyra, she's the youngest of the group. I think she feels she has something to prove so she's always the most serious as well, very focussed. She's pretty nice looking too I guess. Of course you humans all seem enchanted by any of us, but Tyra seems to leave people in a daze. I'm not immune to her looks myself, maybe I'll even ask her out one day. But not yet, she's still quite young; after all she's only eighty two.

My bow and arrows coming flying towards me, I catch them easily.

"C'mon, Leonas is about to brief us". The third member of our hunting group, Ryker, gestures to me.

Ryker is unusual for a faerie, he still has the same pale complexion, but although he's tall he's also fairly broad and well muscled. He's nowhere near as fast as Tyra, (who's the fastest), or even me, but he's much stronger than either of us. I suspect he's got some Orc influence somewhere in his family line, although I'd never tell him that of course.

I head into the next room. Seated at the table in the middle of the room is Leonas and Faye. Although very different, they appear to be having a competition as to who can have the longest hair, Faye with her auburn hair flowing down her back, and Leonas's white beard which currently reaches all the way to his waist, plus a few bonus hairs from his ears, ugghh!

Leonas skips any greeting and begins the briefing. "Faye has seen a vision of a new werewolf within our city, if not stopped it will kill a human and become wild. No doubt it will not take long for the humans to capture it and reveal the magical world currently hidden from them."

I hate werewolves, most other creatures you can try to reason with, but werewolves are driven by pure animal instinct. Here's what you need to know about werewolves.

If a werewolf kills another being it will be turned forever, wild and unreachable. There is no other option when this happens. We would have to kill the creature to save others.

However, within our realm, deep within the Undying Forest, is a community of werewolves. Human by day, they revert to their werewolf state during moonlight, but they have followed a path of enlightenment for centuries until they can control the animal spirit within. If we can capture a new werewolf before they kill, they can be taken to this community to learn their ways.

Leonas finishes his part of the briefing. "Go and stop the werewolf from killing. Faye will give you more details, Faye?"

Faye closes her eyes. "I can see a road, there's an old church, but all the windows seem boarded up." She opens her eyes and looks at us. "Does that help?"

Ryker answers thoughtfully. "That sounds like St Luke's church over on the east side. It's been abandoned for years."

"C'mon then. Let's start there." As usual Tyra is anxious to get on with the job.

We gather the rest of our equipment. For myself I have my bows and arrows and a short sword.

Now you may think that carrying a bow and arrows as well as a short sword by my side would attract attention? No problem, we simply cast a glamour spell, so for me all you'll see is a kid with a hockey stick sticking out of a backpack and a long belt with one end hanging down more than usual.

We head off into the night; we don't use buses or anything like that. Within the shroud of darkness we can run almost unseen, faster than you'd imagine.

"What's the plan?" I ask Ryker. As the eldest he's tasked as being our leader when on patrol.

"I've dipped the tips of our arrows in one of Leonas's potions; it should knock a werewolf out for a few hours, enough to get them out of here and into the Undying Forest."

"Should?" I question.

Ryker smiles, "Don't worry, I'll get you to check."

I grimace at Ryker's dark humour.

"We're nearly there." Tyra's focus is unflappable. "Could be good for us, seems mostly deserted."

Tyra's right, the area is quiet, it appears to be a mix of small industrial units and deserted lots. No one is around at this time of night.

Within a couple more minutes we're on the street Faye described from her visions.

"I'll go high." Tyra runs into an alley and begins jumping between the walls, quickly scaling the heights of the building until she stands atop the roof.

I marvel at her agility. I'm good, but she's just better than anyone I've ever seen.

"I'm going up too" I tell Ryker. I jump high to the first level of a fire escape on the building opposite where Tyra went.

Ryker nods. He heads to cover on the ground; his strength is, well, his strength. It would take him much longer to get up and then down if required.

Within moments I'm on the roof, I head to the edge to watch the street below.

I look over to Tyra. She's perched on the very edge with a balance that sometimes makes me cringe.

The moon is shining brightly with very few clouds, so we have excellent visibility to watch the area.

After more of these patrols than I can remember I settle in for a potentially long night. Faye's visions don't come with a timestamp so it may be hours before our quarry appears. In this case it's about forty minutes later when I catch the tensing of Tyra. She looks over and gestures towards the old church.

I whistle a low note, Ryker looks up and I point towards the church to alert him to our visitor.

Moving carefully along the wall of the church, a shadow creeps out into the moonlight.

Yup, it's a werewolf all right.

Tyra already has her bow out ready, but the werewolf is currently too far away to be sure of a hit, and so far he doesn't know we're here.

I'm tensed, ready to react to anything the werewolf might do, but it's at this point our plans go out the window.

Another shape joins the first werewolf. There are two of them!

I look down at Ryker. He gestures to the first werewolf, then back at myself and Tyra. He then points his spear at the second werewolf.

From experience his meaning is clear. Tyra and I will focus on the first werewolf; Ryker will go for the second one with his spear, also tipped with the knock out potion.

It may seem extreme attacking them with spears and arrows, but werewolves are tough and heal quickly from even extreme wounds. We'll only hurt them temporarily.

I nod at Ryker to confirm I have understood, turning to Tyra I point at myself and her, then at the first werewolf to convey the plan. She nods in acknowledgement and then refocuses back on the werewolves.

The two werewolves are sniffing the air, when the first one suddenly turns his head. He's looking west, back towards the heart of the city. He lets out a low growl and begins to move off. The second werewolf is still staying within the old graveyard.

Ryker waves an arm to indicate we should follow the first werewolf now heading down the road back to the city.

I look at Tyra but she's already seen and is heading across the rooftop of the building to keep the werewolf in sight.

I take a last look at Ryker, he's slowly creeping forward, preparing his attack.

He'll be fine I tell myself as I join Tyra moving quietly

across the rooftop.

The werewolf stops again to sniff the air, Tyra readies her bow again ready to take the shot, but before she can shoot the werewolf is off again.

We jump the gap to the next warehouse, the werewolf still unaware it's being hunted. We just a need a chance to get close enough to take the shot, but whilst we still have the element of surprise we want to maximise the chances of getting a hit, so for now we're not making any snap shots.

I'm starting to get a bad feeling; we're starting to get closer to the city, to people... to trouble.

Up ahead I see a park coming into view, Kingsview Park, I recognise it.

The werewolf stops briefly, sniffing the air intently before leaping into one of the trees at the edge of the park. I recognise the signs. It's hunting.

With a sense of foreboding I scan the park, I chant an incantation and the park zooms into view through enhanced sight.

What has the... there, someone's walking along the paths through the park.

As the person walks under a lamp I see his face clearly, it's a face I recognise, Kyle Redfield. I remember our conversation from earlier, he must be heading over to Henrys house, I can see a bag on his back, no doubt filled with the latest video games.

We need to act quickly now, any hesitation and Kyle will be torn to shreds.

I react on pure instinct, leaping my way down from the roof and heading towards the werewolf, my bow ready. I faintly hear Tyra call out to me, but I don't have time to explain. Besides, I don't want to admit to her that I care for a human.

My feet are almost silent across the ground, when your childhood is spent playing in the forest you learn to move quietly.

As I reach the tree line I begin to ready my bow, creeping ever closer to the werewolf.

I'm not sure what alerts the werewolf, a stray breeze carrying my scent, an almost inaudible sound, maybe pure animal instinct. Whatever it is, as I look at the werewolf I now find myself staring directly into his face; snarling mouth open, eyes locked directly on mine. My blood runs cold.

I snap off a shot from my bow as the werewolf leaps towards me, the arrow brushing past his fur before embedding itself in the tree behind.

In a split second the werewolf reaches me as I fumble frantically for my sword. I can hear Tyra scream behind me as the werewolf slashes its claws towards me. I roll quickly as the claws rip through my backpack holding the rest of my arrows and some schoolwork. Papers fly through the air as I scramble free of the straps and continue to roll. The werewolf grabs my backpack and begins to tear it to bits with his razor sharp teeth, before spitting it out and looking around for a meatier treat… Me!

As I hold my sword before me and prepare for a very one sided fight, I catch sight of Tyra from the corner of my eye as she drops lightly to the ground before bringing up her bow in one smooth motion.

Just as the werewolf is coiled ready to leap at my throat, an arrow from Tyra's bow thuds into the werewolf's back.

With an ear splitting howl the werewolf spins around and begins running towards Tyra.

I can see her eyes go wide as she leaps back to the warehouse, desperately trying to regain a height advantage to keep her away from the now furious beast below.

Dropping my sword I run forward and grab up my bow and a handful of arrows. As Tyra reaches for the roof of the warehouse the werewolf slams into the metal walls, claws ripping into the material, leaving huge scrapes in the sides.

The movement unsettles Tyra and she now hangs by

just one hand, the werewolf snapping at her heels as he leaps towards her.

As fast as I have ever done so I begin firing arrow after arrow at the werewolf, a battle cry roaring from my throat, anything to distract the werewolf from Tyra.

As I fire my final arrow the adrenalin spike wears off as the werewolf turns back towards me. My feet falter as I stop holding my empty bow in front of me.

Flaming witch breath!

I've succeeded all right. The werewolf is focused back on me as I stand there; holding an empty bow, no sword and Tyra still struggling to hold on to the roof above.

It looks like I'm going to be dinner. The werewolf runs towards me, growling. I swing my arm in vain as the werewolf knocks me to the ground and holds me down. Putrid, wet dog-breath fills my nose as the werewolf bares his teeth, ready to take a bite.

As my life flashes before me, the werewolf's eyes suddenly roll back and close, just before the fearsome creature collapses down onto my chest and head.

I can hear footsteps approaching. I struggle to move and look towards the sound as Ryker's shoes suddenly fill my vision not blocked by fur.

"Looks like I do all the work while you're lying here just having a rest."

"Just get this thing off me!" I reply.

Tyra suddenly joins Ryker.

"You got the other one?" She enquires, always focussed, ignoring my plight, stuck beneath the huge weight crushing down on me.

"No problems. Although the potion took a bit longer to take effect than planned."

I groan. No kidding.

"Hello? Anyone want to help me?"

Ryker grabs my arms and pulls me from under the sleeping werewolf.

I stand up and dust myself off as the other two grin at me.

Tyra reaches out and punches my arm lightly. "Thanks for saving me. Though it wasn't much of a plan."

"You're welcome." I reply, ignoring the part about my lack of planning.

"So what are we doing with sleeping beauty, and where's the other one?"

Ryker gestures down the path. "His friend's back down the path behind a tree. I'll go get him. You open the portal." Ryker hands over a bag of sand before heading back down the path.

With my breath now back to normal I check around to ensure we were still alone, with the coast clear I pull out a handful of the sand and gently throw some into the air whilst chanting the portal spell.

There is a slight breeze as before us grows a doorway into the Faerie Realm. Tyra blows gently on a horn, and within a few minutes a pair of werewolves appear on the other side of the portal. The werewolves bow their heads; these are inhabitants from the Undying Forest. As Ryker approaches, struggling with his werewolf, the other werewolves step through cautiously, sniffing the air.

Then without any apparent effort they each take one of the werewolves and step back through the portal, taking the pair to their village where they will teach them to master their animal instincts. As the portal begins to close, they bow again towards us, and we return the bow.

"Good work!" Ryker announces, before nodding towards me. "Although try not to get so personal next time!"

Tyra giggles as Ryker continues. "Okay, make sure you've got everything and let's head home."

Home. What a great idea. I'm tired and sore from my encounter. I head over to pickup my things and gather up the remains of my backpack.

As I survey the damage my heart sinks.

Oh great, my carefully completed homework is in tatters, I'll have to stay up late to get it done for tomorrow. After all, what could I tell My Philkins?

'Sorry sir, a werewolf ate my homework!'

The Brigglenannocks
By Andrew Merson

Late at night, when the stars shine bright
And Christmas Eve is all but done,
Those impish fiends the size of beans
The Brigglenannocks come.

They'll scare a mouse, destroy a house,
And all in thirty seconds flat,
They come in droves, from dark dank groves,
Riding a domestic cat.

They go on raids with sharpened blades
Cutting stockings from the mantelpiece
So girls and boys just lose their toys
Lying in their beds at peace:

A horrid way to start Christmas Day
It will never be the same
As the time you woke, took a look, and choked:
The Brigglenannocks came!

When I was a boy, there was no joy
In our village for years on end
Those evil gnomes destroyed our homes
Without a buck in trend.

Tired and weary, December was dreary,
We nearly called a Christmas ban
Until one year, amidst the fear
I came up with a plan.

Though it was great, it was too late,
To save the Christmas coming
But as a team, we'd plan the scheme
To send the Brigglenannocks running.

We didn't wait to choose the bait
We picked it with the greatest ease
For what they like, those little tykes
Is stinking, fetid, rancid cheese.

We'd pour some glue on Danish blue
And leave it scattered around the dell
They'd take a lick, their tongues would stick
And then we'd throw them down the well.

In one fell swoop, we'd get the group,
The plan was just so fiendishly clever.
They'd all be gone by Christmas dawn
We'd live our lives in peace forever.

From New Year's Day to the first of May
The cows were milked by the whole village
Our thought the same, our common aim:
To cease the Brigglenannocks pillage.

Much to his shock we cleared the stock
From the Quartermaster's Shop
For it would hold the dairy mould
We'd fill it right up to the top.

Two hundred days of cheesy haze
It was the smelliest ever chore
But by November, as I remember,
We'd filled the Quartermaster's store.

We made our fare with days to spare
But one last task we'd have to leave
The sabotage of our fromage
Would have to wait till Christmas Eve.

The twenty-fourth: we ventured forth
The sight of the storeroom struck us dumb
Those evil brutes had smelled our loot
And stolen every last crumb.

Tempers were hot, morale was shot,
Things would just remain the same,
So late that night, when the stars shone bright
The Brigglenannocks came.

They come in droves, from dark dank groves,
Swarming like a hive of bees
They'd stop and grin, to rub it in
Snacking on the stolen cheese.

And on that night, to their delight
The stockings were full of cheddar and gouda
But to their displeasure, as a countermeasure
We'd covered the cheeses with itching powder.

Some of them scowled, some of them howled
One of them just dropped down dead
They itched and rubbed and scratched and scrubbed
Until their skin was red.

Badly burned, they never returned,
And Christmases come without any panic.
But you might catch a glimpse of one of those imps -
Was that a Brigglenannock?

Deep Within a Forest
By J.R. Troughton

It was a summer evening when I died.

I had been playing with a handful of local boys and girls in the park near to my house for most of the day. I didn't know any of them particularly well, having only moved to the village a fortnight previously, but they seemed friendly enough. They had all gone home early for one reason or another, be it for an early dinner or to carry out their chores, leaving me to my own devices late in the afternoon. The air was warm and inviting and the smell of cut grass invigorated me. Rather than go home myself, I decided to properly explore my new home.

The village itself was small. Nothing but an extended t-junction, really, with less than 200 people living there. I had seen the entirety of the village by now of course, but I had always fancied myself as an explorer and decided to investigate further. I set off walking down the empty street running by the old church, kicking pebbles to the curb and stretching my arms to embrace the afternoon air.

As I walked, the houses slowly died off to be replaced by bramble thickets and nettles as high as my shoulder. The road itself steadily warped away, the tarmac changed to earth and tufts of grass. Trees lined the dirt path, dropping a blanket of shadow and leaning over me like a series of overfriendly relations.

Time passed and I continued to walk. In truth, I could hardly have gone further than a mile or two, but it felt like I was discovering a whole new world. By now the trees had largely given way too. To one side of me was a field of golden corn that stretched off into the summer haze and the other was, still, a wall of brambles that came to well over my shoulder. The sun was starting to slink away into the horizon now but the warmth of the day continued as my path began to slope downwards. My face was sticky from hours of play and my journey into the wilds of the world had my legs aching.

The going was easier now I was moving downhill. The corn field had been replaced by more brambles and looming trees, and I was now surrounded by thick foliage. Insects were whizzing and spinning around my head, dodging my flailing hands to irritate my ears and eyes and mouth. It was like I had gone back in time. Civilisation did not exist for me. I was a boy uncovering a hidden and undiscovered world. As I continued further, however, my journey soon stalled.

I had come across a river, murky dark and covered thick with lilies. Giant blue and red dragonflies skimmed the surface, searching for whatever hidden treasure it is dragonflies seek, and a small bird hopped to and fro on the far bank. Across the river lay a deep forest. The only way across was a long iron girder, lying on its side, spanning bank to bank. Taking a deep breath, I stepped onto the girder, grasped the ridged top with my hands, and slowly shimmied my way across. Pausing halfway, I looked down the river. It stretched far away before curving back into the forest. A giant green and blue dragonfly hovered in front of my face, considered me for a moment, before flitting away to a distant lily. I continued.

Stepping off the girder at the far end, I wiped my grimy hands against my shorts. My knuckles were ghost-white; I hadn't realised how hard I had been gripping the girder. Grinning to myself and shaking the white away, I peered into the trees. Now I was on the cusp of the forest, I realised there was no obvious path, so I simply ducked into the trees and made my own way.

It was not long before I considered myself lost. This didn't upset me, for all great explorers must get lost from time to time, but it did frustrate that I wasn't sure which way I should be heading and which way adventure lay. I was covered in a blanket of shade from the trees, with the dying sun only showing through rare gaps in the canopy. I continued on, realising I would not have long before I would have to turn around and head for home.

Hearing a long and screeching birdcall I did not recognize, my eyes lifted to the roof of leaves above. As I scanned the trees for the mysterious bird, my foot caught on a thick root, sending me tumbling into the detritus of the forest floor. Pine needles stabbed at my knees and, as I tried to catch myself, I dragged my elbow hard across a rock. Yelping with pain, I sat up and inspected my arm. The scrape was about the same size as a playing card, ash white, with diamonds of crimson rapidly swelling. Pulling a tissue from my pocket I pressed against the cut, wincing as hot needles stung at my arm. Anger welled up in me and I kicked my foot back at the offending tree root. This led to a second yelp, my foot connecting with something hard which gave no purchase, no matter how great my anger was.

Scrunching up my eyes in pain and irritation, I shuffled forward and brushed away the fallen needles, leaves and earth that covered the root. To my surprise I found it was not a root at all, but what seemed to be a curved metal pipe, about three inches thick, rusted and stained by the soil. Following the pipe with my hands, I clumsily shovelled away the decaying leaves,

What I found was unexpected. It was a foot. A foot made of metal, sure, but a foot all the same. It seemed overly large, about the length of two bricks, and there were only four toes, small thimble sized pieces of corroded steel. Excitement bubbled within me and my digging quickened. Scrabbling at the earth I followed the leg towards where I assumed the body would lie. It was against the trunk of a thick oak tree, covered by decomposing leaves, pine needles and a thin layer of emerald moss. The moss itself was dry and weak from the long heat of the summer and scraps came away as I brushed off the debris.

It was not long before I had nearly uncovered the entire thing. It was a dark, rusty brown in colour, basically human in shape, though with limbs that were double the length they would have been if it were human. If standing I imagined it to have been close to twice my height. The body was slim, though given a degree of girth by the haphazard clumps of moss that clung to it. Its single hand – the other was missing, its wrist a mess of faded and split red, blue and yellow wires – was the size and shape of a tennis ball, with four long fingers standing rigid and to attention. Peeling the thin mask of moss away from the head, I found the thing did not have a face. Instead was a single large glass lens, concave in shape and black in colour. There was a jagged crack running about three quarters of the way across it, from the upper-left towards the lower right.

I sat back in awe. I had found, and in my mind there could be no mistake, a robot. It was lifeless, rusting and abandoned; a sorry kind of robot for sure, but a robot nonetheless. My arm was still oozing blood, the entire scrape now a reddish-pink, but the pain barely registered. My heart and brain raced one another.

The light was fading fast but I knew I could not leave my discovery as it was. Mother and dinner would have to wait, no matter what awful punishment would be dished out. Crawling back over to the robot, I brushed the rest of the moss from its head, cleared its chest and inspected it further. The large cylindrical chest seemed to have a compartment on the front, and a quick knock showed it was hollow inside. As for the head, I found two things of interest. On the rear of the rusted cranium was a rectangular black and white counter that read '**027**', and, underneath that, a small button with a lightning strike embossed upon it. My heart beat faster still – Could this be a power button? The counter, and its mysterious number, was all but forgotten as I stared intently at the circular switch.

I pressed it.

Nothing happened.

Then, after a few moments of waiting, a loud and steady clicking started to emanate from the robot. Slowly at first, perhaps once every three or four seconds, then faster and faster still. By the time it was clicking every second, I had ducked behind a nearby tree to watch from a safer distance. The clicks turned to a whirr as they melded into one another and the glass lens started to flash. First purple and red, then blue and green, before freezing on a thick mustard yellow. I chewed at my lip and watched as the robot suddenly sat up. It did not move for the next minute or so, and neither did I. Then, as quickly as it had sat up, it rose to its feet and started to walk in the opposite direction to my hiding spot, moving gracefully and with surprising speed.

I followed from a distance.

Every so often the robot would stop and appear to study its surroundings, turning its head left and right and sometimes reaching out with its solitary hand to grasp at a tree or rock or bush. It never stayed still for more than about 15 seconds though, before rapidly moving on at a high pace. I was starting to get hungry now and the wood was growing uncomfortably dark. Looking over my shoulder and into the darkness behind me; how was I going to find my way back? I continued to follow the eerie eye into the woods. There was almost no light now barring the pallid radiance coming from the Cyclops. It was enchanting, bobbing gently up and down and appearing to hang in the air, the body hidden by darkness. I could make out a number of mosquitoes flicking around its head, drawn in by the glow. The nearby twitter of an owl seemed to catch the attention of the robot, whose head rotated sharply sideways and quickened its step as it approached a tree. It raised its arms and reached up towards where the sound had come from. They extended rapidly and silently. A faint rustling told me the owl was flying away into the night, and I looked on curiously as the cable arms slowly retracted.

The robot paused for a few moments, before striding off into the wood once more. I kept pace.

I was quickly running out of breath now. The robot was fast and rarely stopped for more than a few seconds. Taking a moment to gather myself, I leant against a tree, closed my eyes and took a deep breath.

Opening my eyes, I turned back to the robot and my legs wobbled. It had turned and was facing directly towards me, the glowing yellow orb unblinking and unyielding. I cowered behind the tree, poking my head out just enough to see if it was coming my way. It was, and fast.

In the daylight the robot had seemed like a fantastic discovery, a one in a million kind of thing that I was lucky to find, but now dusk had come and the bleak night had enveloped the woods?

Fear was creeping up my spine and sweat beading on my forehead. My arm was stinging more and more too.

My mind scrambled, frantically trying to decide on a course of action, but the robot appeared in front of me before I did so. The yellow glow of the eye burnt into my retinas. I brought my arm up to protect them. Turning to run, the coarse grip of the rusted fingers clamped around my forearm, pressing against the graze. I screamed.

Pulling me effortlessly towards him, the robots eye briefly flashed red. The door on its chest slowly swung open and I winced as I recognized the shapes tumbling out as broken bones. A skull thudded across the forest floor. The robotic arm dragged me closer, pulling me agonisingly off the floor and towards the tomb in its chest. The compartment wasn't large and, as I realised my fate, my screaming hit fever pitch. Pushing me as far as I would go into the compartment, ignoring my screams and futile kicks, the robot's handless arm pinned me to the back. My head was bent forward, my arms bent back, the only parts of my body not inside were my legs. Seizing them with his iron grip, the robot snapped my legs back awkwardly and slammed the door. I passed out in a broken mess.

The robot turned and marched away into the darkness.

The counter ticked slowly.

[028]

And that was the day I died.

Billy Fredericks
By Andrew Merson

Billy sat in his room looking at his laptop screen. The internet browser showing a Wikipedia page was now in the background, having given way to his instant messenger. There was a healthy list of names with green dots next to them, Billy had enough friends that there were always half a dozen online, but as usual he was chatting to just one: Pippa.

Billy Fredericks and Pippa Harding had been friends since their first day at school. Mrs. Fredericks often hoped that as they grew older it would be more than that, but Billy never seemed to talk about her that way. It was as though they'd been friends from too young an age for that to happen. They were best friends, and that was that.

Billy and Pippa had gone through the topics they always covered on their nightly chats; the latest moron to audition for X Factor, who fancied who at school, YouTube links of their current favourite Belle & Sebastian track, and swapping funny pictures of anthropomorphised cats. Now they were onto something that genuinely worried them - choosing their subjects for the next two years.

Pippa was more or less set, and just had to pick between Biology or Geography for the final slot. She'd already chosen History and Chemistry, but the decision to take two social sciences or two actual sciences was increasingly looking like it would be decided by the toss of a coin. Pippa knew that was no way to start your future, but she occasionally let herself give in to Billy's more relaxed ideas.

Billy, on the other hand, was lost. He had a vague idea that he wanted to study something academically sexy at university, something that would let him wear a long coat in summer, read battered paperbacks by French philosophers while smoking a rolled up cigarette and drinking coffee, but he wasn't entirely sure what route he would take to get there. He was too afraid to admit this secret ambition to Pippa, so when she pressed him about his choices he opted for his usual response.

i dunno

> *well, ud better decide soon, billy*
> *weve only got another week 2 hand in the forms*
> *anyway am going 2 bed*

yeah
i will
here, check this video, pip

> *am going 2 bed*

ok, well look at this pic then

> *lol*
> *am going 2 bed*

fair enuff
sorry
maybe you cn help me with the form 2moz?
> *sure*
> *nunight billy xoxox*

night pip
sweet dreams

may urs come tru billy

    Billy looked out of his window and watched a meteor trace its final path across the sky. He closed the laptop, jamming his notepad with scribbled notes against the keyboard, put it onto the floor and rolled into bed, the light of his phone illuminating his face under the duvet.

Billy woke as he bounced off his bed, thumped onto the carpet and hit his head on his laptop, cracking the lid.

"Ow!"

He looked around him, dazed, working out where he was. He looked at his laptop, swore, and rubbed his temple. He was relieved to find that the screen was still working. His dad would've killed him if he'd broken it; this was his second one, the first having been replaced after it was left on the floor and trodden on. It was actually Pippa who broke it, but even she knew she wasn't to blame for that one.

Billy climbed back into bed. He'd had that dream where you're suddenly falling, and you wake up just before you hit the ground. He must've flailed so wildly that he'd fallen off the edge of the mattress. He pulled the duvet back over himself, and tried to ignore the carpet burn on the side of his hand.

Mr. Fredericks dropped the top of his newspaper enough to watch Billy walk into the dining room.

"What, pray tell, was that noise last night?"

"I fell out of bed," muttered Billy as he grabbed a slice of toast from the table and headed out the front door.

"I made you eggs, Bil... oh," sighed Mrs. Fredericks as she carried a frying pan in from the kitchen. "Where has he gone?"

"He fell out of bed," announced Mr. Fredericks, not looking up from his paper.

"When? What? Is he away? Frank?" Mr. Fredericks flicked the newspaper, flattening the column he was reading and drawing her attention to the fact that he was busy in one swift movement. "Never mind."

Billy looked at his class, and his class looked back at him. They were all laughing, except for Pippa, who was covering her mouth and blushing.

"What's so funny?" Billy thought to himself. He hadn't done as much research as he should have for his talk on the Sea of Tranquillity, but he didn't think it was that bad. It certainly wasn't half as shoddy as Jake McLeod's talk. He actually believed that the moon was the same thing as the sun, but it got 'turned down' because it was night time.

With that, Billy felt a breeze. He looked down, and realised why everyone was laughing. Billy was completely naked.

"It's okay," he said to himself, "it's just a dream. Everyone has this dream. I'll pinch myself. *Ow!* Try harder. *OW!*"

By now, Sonia and Lauren were pointing at him, their false nails keeping steady aim even while they giggled and gasped at each other in false innocence. Pippa was climbing under her desk in shame.

Ms. Goodfellow had not been paying attention for some time, staring out the window, still trying to formulate the second chapter of the novel she had been working on for the last twenty three years. At first she had ignored the laughter - Billy was always keen to entertain his classmates - but as the room descended into chaos, her focus was pulled back to the room, to the fourteen year old boy at the front, and the A4 pad which was the only thing protecting his modesty.

"William Fredericks, what on *earth* are you playing at?" she demanded, in her usual clipped manner.

"Its okay, miss, I'll wake up any minute," he offered, hopefully, but this didn't feel like a dream, and as he sat outside the headmaster's office he wondered where, exactly, his clothes had gone.

On Friday morning, walking to school, nobody would talk to Billy, except Pippa. Even then, 'talking' was a bit of an overstatement. In fairness, given yesterday's events, walking next to him in slightly hostile silence was about as good as he could hope for. She was his best friend, and she would forgive him eventually, but for now he would have to pay for mortifying her.

"...I don't even know what happened, I still haven't found my trousers, these are my dad's old work ones, and it wasn't like I was worried about my talk, Ms. Goodfellow wasn't even paying attention..." Billy had been going over and over the incident, as though he might somehow happen upon an answer, but deep down he knew it was hopeless. The closer he got to school, the more he was sure other kids were looking and grinning. Stories like that don't disappear, and last night someone had set up a facebook page that now had over a thousand 'likes'. He'd been up all night trying to report the page to the admins, but they'd just laughed at him. Today was going to be hell, and it would start with double history.

Mr. Clarke was standing by the whiteboard, dry-wipe marker in hand, his voice droning like the engines of the B52s he was describing with absolutely no enthusiasm, making the bombing of Dresden sound like the dullest, most soporific thing to happen since, well, anything else Mr. Clarke had ever taught.

The blast launched desks across the classroom, the shattered glass of the windows flying through the air like deadly confetti. As the smoke still billowed about the room, the screams gradually faded to whimpers. Billy pushed away the desk that had landed on him, reached around and found Pippa's hand, which gripped his and clearly wasn't letting go. In the darkness he slowly shifted the rubble she was buried under. Around him, he could make out the figures of his pals dusting themselves off, digging each other out. Mr. Clarke was found cowering at the feet of his silhouette, the only area of whiteboard not scorched by the explosion.

Amazingly, no one was badly hurt. Even more astonishing was the fact that, as the fire brigade had found from the wreckage, when the school was built on top of an unexploded World War II bomb, it had neither been

65

discovered nor activated. Somehow it had been triggered on a quiet Friday morning, but nobody quite knew how.

That night, as Billy and Pippa sat on the swings, Billy felt the words he wanted to say forming in his mouth, but somehow he couldn't, no, he *daren't* actually say them out loud.

"You know something about the explosion, don't you?" asked Pippa, apparently out of nowhere. Billy didn't know whether to be relieved that he didn't have to bring it up, or freaked out that she knew what he was thinking.

"What makes you say that?"

"You've been acting funny. Ever since it happened you've been... weird."

"I think everyone has been a bit weird, Pip. It was a weird thing to happen."

"You've been weirder, though. And you were already acting pretty strange."

Billy flashed her a look. "Thanks, Pippa. Who needs enemies..."

"You're my best friend, Billy, but if you had something to do with that, I'll have to tell the Police. You could've killed us."

"I didn't do it deliberately!"

"So it *was* you."

"No! Yes. Maybe. I dunno."

"You'd better explain why, Billy. Make it good and make it quick, because I don't think I want to be around you right now."

"I think my dreams are coming true."

"What? You're sick."

"No, not like that. Not the phrase. I think my *actual* dreams are *actually* coming true. I dream something, and it happens."

"Sod off, Billy." Pippa shrugged herself off her swing

and started to walk away.

"Wait! Are you telling me you've never had the dream where you haven't done your homework, or you're suddenly naked in front of all your friends? I had that dream and suddenly there I was, it was happening."

"Really?". Pippa stopped and turned. "And what about the rest of the day, Billy? I was there! You weren't asleep. How could your dream 'suddenly' happen if you were wide awake?"

"I dunno. It just... It just did."

"Piss off, Billy Fredericks. Don't speak to me ever again."

Billy stood alone in the park and watched as she ran off, sobbing.

Billy sat on his bed, pressed into the corner, his knees tucked up into his chest, his hands clasped onto his shins, and concentrated on staying awake. Whatever happened, he mustn't fall asleep. He must stay awake. Must... stay... awake... Must... stay...

Billy sprinted down the supermarket aisle, tins and jars blasting off the shelves as he ran, his invisible pursuant never quite catching up.

"This is ridiculous!" he screamed, at nobody in particular. This was the supermarket in the town centre that his mum used to take him to as a child. She'd stopped when the Tesco had opened up near the by-pass, and Billy hadn't been back since. He couldn't really remember what it looked like, but this was definitely it,
and for some reason it was now next door to his house, and had things in it that wanted to hurt him.

Billy ducked around a corner, pressed his back against the shelves, and peered back around at where he had just come from. The floor was covered in spilled food and exploded packaging. Climbing down from the shelves was, well, something. Billy couldn't quite focus on it, it was always just to one side of where he was looking, but it was there. A presence. A can of pears in syrup whistled past his face, and it was time to run again.

He burst through the store room doors which for reasons he couldn't explain brought him from the back of the shop to the fruit and veg displays, careering headlong toward the front door. As he willed it to happen, two melons flew over his shoulders and smashed through the glass on the automatic doors, and Billy dove
through, skidding to a halt on the pavement.

"That's breaking and entering, and a pretty serious amount of vandalism," said the Policeman, looking down at Billy.

"Oh, and shoplifting," joked the Policewoman, removing pick'n'mix from Billy's hair.

"Wh-what?" stammered Billy. "No, that wasn't me. The thing, it was trying to kill me."

The cops looked at each other and sighed. It would be nice if once, just once, one of these kids wasn't a liar.

"I mean, I'm not sure what it was, but it was throwing stuff at me."

Or mental.

"Aren't either of you bothered that this shop shouldn't be here? It's meant to be on the High Street."

Or both. The Policeman grabbed Billy's collar, and hauled him to his feet.

"Alright sunshine," he growled, "let's get you back to the office and we'll phone your mum."

The next night, Billy sat in his room. He'd been there all day. His mum said he could come down for lunch, and had pleaded with him to come down for dinner, but he just sat and stared at the wall. His TV, Xbox, and laptop were out in his dad's shed. He was stuck in his bedroom for the rest of the weekend, and all week, and no doubt the next weekend too.

Normally he wouldn't mind, he had plenty reading to catch up on, but stories of wizards wouldn't take his mind off the crazy turn his life had taken. He also didn't want to read about it in case he dreamt about it. He was too scared to look at anything.

He heard the muffled sound of the back door being knocked, and voices in the kitchen. It was Pippa. As he heard her chat with his mum end, and her footsteps come up the stairs, he wasn't sure it was safe to see her. What if he dreamt something bad happened to her? He wouldn't mean to, but now they had argued it was more likely to happen, no matter how much he wouldn't want to.

A tentative knock, and his door edged open. Pippa's face appeared in the gap. She was clearly concerned, but she forced a smile.

"Your mum asked me to come and see you."

"I'm not sure that's a good idea."

"Well, sometimes it's good to talk. Get things off your chest."

"I take it you heard about the supermarket?"

"It would be hard not to."

"Pippa, how long has that shop been there?"

"It's been open since before we were born. I think some of the food has been there since it opened!" she joked, trying to raise a smile. "I mean, who actually eats tinned potatoes these days?!"

"Yes, but how long has it been *there*. On this street."

"Always. Billy, you're worrying me."

"Are you *sure*?"

Pippa stopped in her tracks, and looked into Billy's eyes. She had been sure, until he'd questioned it. Now it seemed... odd. She wasn't sure why, couldn't place her finger on it. She probably just wanted to believe him, she thought. Probably. But then... no, that was silly.

"Billy, I think you're just stressing about picking subjects. You haven't had enough sleep."

"I don't want to sleep. If I sleep I will dream, and if I

dream, who knows what will happen?"

"I'll stay here with you. It'll be ok."

"Pippa, please, no!" Billy broke down. She'd never seen him like this. She sat next to him on the bed, and put her arm around him. He slumped into her, then slouched down and rested his head on her knees, quietly crying as she stroked his hair.

"Please don't let me fall asleep, Pip," he begged. She agreed, he made her promise, but she had no intention of keeping it. He needed rest. And maybe he was right. Maybe his dreams *were* coming true.

As his breathing slowed and deepened, she leaned down and whispered in his ear.

"Dream that we fall in love, Billy."

Pippa looked out the window and watched a meteor trace its final path across the sky.

The Ylenolians
By Andrew Merson

Of all the folk in Ylenol, the saddest is the Ylenol Yob;
brought up by El Baresim, he didn't know about human touch.

Ylenol is full of fearful folk, who speak not of that
beyond their town. For in the woods live beasts, they say, that
live on Ylenol's broken hearts.

The first of these terrifying things is a creature called
Devolnu Retsnom. They say it's never had a friend, or
laughed along with another.

The other is more ghastly, yet they dare not mumble
why. Doots Red Nusim is its name, and hell comes with its
reputation

Quite wily were these wicked things, quite cunning in
their art. They skulked around just out of sight; an ever
present threat.

For fourteen years they held their nerve, the Ylenolians
said, not once in that time striking forth - but if they did, oh, if
they did…

And so it was, that fateful day, when the Ylenol Yob
set forth. El Baresim had had enough, the Yob must leave,
must go at once.

And as the Yob walked through the town, nobody saw
him pass, for wrapped in fear, the people were, at what might
happen next.

Who knew when Retsnom would next strike, or what
his opening move would be, and would they hear Red
Nusim's roar, that made them all despair?

The Yob walked on, with little choice, the town grew
small behind him, and yet, with every step he took he found
his heart felt lighter.

The trees grew thick, drew close together, and vines
pulled on the Yob's clothes, but through the trees he saw a
light, and smelt a smell as sweet as heaven.

Beyond the trees he found a meadow, with flowers of

the yellowest yellow, and there, skipping beside a stream: Devolnu Retsnom, singing.

Doots Red Nusim appeared just then, at the door of a little cottage, and offered the Ylenol Yob a drink, of freshly squashed banana.

They looked on him with cautious eyes, scared of what they saw, for if he was what they thought he was, it would change their lives forever.

Are you from within the trees? The place that once did prosper? It turned so dark, it turned away, it is the place where anger lies.

The Yob felt born again, he knew he'd found his home, he'd not return from whence he came, for death lay in that darkness.

The Diary of Henry Nicholas, Boy Genius
By Chris Preece

*The following diary extracts were passed on to us by The
Academy for Incredibly Gifted Children. They inform us that
they were received anonymously, with a hand written letter
that simply read, "By way of explanation for my absence".
They have declined to comment on the document's
authenticity.*

December 16th

    My Dad is *so* embarrassing. Seriously. You know
what he's done this time? He's got a job as a Santa
impersonator. Red hat, fat suit, the lot. He's going to be
handing out toys at Jamieson's Department Store, sat in a
plastic sleigh, surrounded by women dressed as elves. If
anyone from the Academy sees him, I'll never hear the end of
it. It's bad enough being the scholarship boy, the one with the
uniform two sizes too small, and the permanently scuffed
shoes. The postman's kid. If they find out my Dad's
moonlighting as Father Christmas I'm dead.
    Idiot. Why now? When I'm so close? I'm right on
the cusp of mastering time and space itself. Will anyone care?
No, they'll be too busy making jokes about mistletoe and
asking where the reindeer are. I mean, I get it, I know my
equipment's not cheap. I know that. I understand why he felt
he had to get a second job, and I'm grateful. Honestly. Just
not this one. Why couldn't he do something where no-one
would see him? Work in a call centre or something?
Anything, that doesn't involve him spending hours practicing
his "ho ho ho" all evening?
    Still, at least the experiment's going well. I managed
to figure out a way to stabilise the Electrical Latency Field, by
feeding back the temporal interface. It looks, on paper at
least, like it should be able to hold within whatever

parameters I set. I had to cheat a little bit, I've set the temporal relay along the line of a simple calendar year, subdivided into 24 hour units, and then individual one hour divisions. Just to keep it simple. (I used the Gregorian model, inserting Leap Years, just for fun.)   Obviously once I'm completely satisfied with the field I can experiment with more complex temporal arrays.

Not that anyone will notice, they'll probably just ask me if they're on the naughty list…

December 17th

He's brought home some reindeer. They're out in the back yard right now, munching on straw. Two of them, and yes, one of them is called Rudolph. Apparently the store got them in to attract the kids, but have been told it's against Health and Safety to leave them there overnight. Madness - I've told him to stop, told him what I think, he just winked, and told me he's going to be the best Santa ever.   Perhaps I should ring the council, I'm sure they're no more allowed round here than they are at Jamieson's.

You'd think he would at least have the decency to pretend that he's no happier about it than I am, but no. He loves it. He's always loved Christmas, my Dad. He's obsessed with it. When I was younger he would always go on about the last Christmas he spent with my Mum, not long before I was born. He used to pretend that Father Christmas himself turned up on Christmas Eve, arms filled with presents. (Always "Father Christmas" – "That's the real one son," he would insist, "Santa's the name he gives to his helpers.") It was a good story, always told with a glint in his eye. The young couple, no money, no food, baby on the way, and suddenly a knock on the door, and there's the man himself, straight out of a story book. The gifts were all perfect ("that's where we got Mr Cuddles from"), and St Nick and his elfin helper set about cooking Christmas dinner, as if they had nothing better to do. "Best day of my life that was, son, best day of my life."

All the other parents I know say that about the birth of their children, but I guess Dad has his reasons not to.

Still, I shall try and concentrate on my work. Soon I think I'll be ready to try and test out the field.

December 18th

Well, that was confusing.

This morning I awoke to find a digital timer sat in the middle of the Field Generator. That in itself isn't surprising: the plan had been to buy one today, place it in the generator at 8am tomorrow morning, and set the temporal relay for -1day thus essentially sending it back in time. So the presence of the watch is good news. The Field works, Nobel prizes await, and the Academy for Incredibly Gifted Children will find its decision to offer me a scholarship vindicated. Hooray for me.

Except, there's something about the stopwatch I don't understand. I wanted a watch, because I needed to test whether there was any time lag, anything lost when I sent it back, that might imply I've miscalibrated. There was, I think. What I don't understand is how much. The display on the counter had maxed out completely - all 9s across the entire screen. 99,999,999 seconds, that's 1,157 days. Over 3 years. That's a massive miscalculation for something that still managed to turn up at precisely 8:00am.

Yet, that wasn't the strangest thing. The strangest thing was that the battery seemed to be pretty much fully charged. After 3 years.

I've spent the rest of the day trying to figure out what I got wrong, so much so that I almost forgot to run out and get the timer. I'm no closer to figuring out what happened, but I'll send it off tomorrow morning as planned.

December 19th

I sent the timer. I've double-checked everything, all of the settings were correct. It should have gone back exactly one day. It did, I just can't explain the other stuff. The job's not made any easier by Dad singing Christmas songs all day. I pointed out that, actually, we don't all like figgy pudding, but he just stuck out his tongue and called me a Scrooge.

This isn't the only reason that I'm in a bad mood, I spent half the day searching for the timer, to try and inspect it more closely, but I can't remember where I left it. The only proof I have for what happened to it are my notes from yesterday. That Nobel prize may have to wait a little longer.

December 20th

It's happened. Julie Finchley saw my Dad. The Julie Finchley - from school. Highest ranked IQ in the world, leading wormhole theorist, inventor of Finchley's Inverted Quantum Law and DREAM GIRL. According to Dad she didn't just see him, he actually waved to her and shouted her name. He spent the whole evening trying to persuade me that this wasn't the long lingering social death it clearly is. Every reassuring platitude just rammed another nail into the coffin of my self-respect. "Don't worry Henry, she loved it. She even came over and told me her Christmas list, though I had to admit I didn't really know what a particle accelerator was…"

That's it. I'll have to quit the Academy, there's nothing else for it. I don't get anything out of it anyway, Prof Carruthers all but admitted that the Electrical Latency Temporal Flow theory was beyond him. I can never show my face again. Never.

December 21st

Dad's been acting all hurt because I've been refusing to speak to him after the Finchley Incident. It's his own fault, I warned him, and now he's ruined my life. RUINED.

I still can't find the timer. I bet that's his fault too, the reindeer have probably eaten it.

December 22nd

Right then. It was obviously a mistake to send the timer back in time. This time I'm going to experiment with going the other way round. I've managed to send one forwards to tomorrow. It disappeared in the expected fashion, so here's hoping the readout's not gone haywire this time.

Meanwhile, Dad's trying to get back in my good books. A present has appeared under the tree – evidently I'm supposed to be excited. Doubtless it'll be another "Kitchen Science" set or similar such nonsense, I sometimes wonder if he has any grasp of what I'm doing at all.

December 23rd

99999999 seconds. No loss of battery power. No explanation. It makes literally no sense to me at all.

Dad came home and put on his Christmas CD, the one he plays every year. I cracked about half way through "Merry Xmas Everybody" and snapped it in half. I felt a bit guilty really, but I can't think with someone shouting, "It's Chriiiiiiiiiistmas!!!!" in the background. I'll burn him a new copy once I've solved this problem. If I solve this problem.

December 24th

The second timer's disappeared as well. Obviously Dad's taken it in revenge for the CD thing. He's like a spoiled child sometimes. I confronted him about it, but he denied everything, told me I must have lost it.

I haven't lost it. I know exactly where I left it, because I didn't move it. If it's not there, he must have taken it.

Still, shouldn't have said what I said. That was unfair, that was… cruel, I suppose. That's the problem with family, you always know exactly what to say to get to them. I didn't mean it, not a word, though I know he meant his reply.

I said I wished he'd died instead of Mum. He said, "So do I".

He's not come home yet, I wish he would. I want to say sorry.

Why didn't he just tell me what he'd done with the timer?

December 25th

I've made a decision. I don't know if it will work, but I have to try. I'm going to put myself in the Electrical Latency Field. I'm going to go back in time. I'm going to fix what I've done.

Dad's dead.

He crashed the car. Right after he left. He was going too fast, hit some ice and smashed into the massive Christmas Tree in town. If that had been anyone else, I would think it was funny. I'm a horrible person.

I went and opened my present. It was a brand new digital timer.

My Dad's dead, and it's all my fault, and I have to make it better.

So I'm going to set the field for -1 day. If everything works, I can go back in time and stop him. If it fails, then I'm dead, and I won't care anymore.

Goodbye.

December 24th Ver. 2

I'm alive!

A couple of interesting observations. Firstly, there's just one of me. I wasn't sure if I'd have a double when I got here, but no. I have no idea how that works. I just appeared in the spot I was stood at this time yesterday/today. (It's confusing.)

The day's gone really well. I made Dad a replacement copy of his CD, and just spent the whole day enjoying his company. He's still an idiot, but he's alright really. We sang silly songs, and fed the stupid reindeer.

We did not fight. He's downstairs right now watching "It's a Wonderful Life". Seriously. He's going to live.

Oh, and I've invented a fully operational time machine. I can't wait for tomorrow.

December 24th Ver. 3

I know what happened to the timers. If only I'd worked it out. If only I'd spent a bit more time understanding what I'd made.

Dad didn't take the timers, and the reindeer haven't eaten them. They're right *where* I left them. They're right *when* I left them.

The timers maxed out to 99999999 because they had been stuck in an infinite loop. They got through their 24 hours then looped straight back to the start. But the numbers kept running until the display was filled. The battery resets, their physical position resets, but the numbers keep on running. It's something, I think, to do with the nature of observation. The act of counting is somehow a form of observation it carries out on itself, an internal check, and the latency field doesn't alter that. There must be something functioning at a quantum level that I don't understand. I'm not sure even Julie Finchley could explain it to me.

I know this, because the same thing's happening to me.

It's the same day again. I remember the last one. I remember everything up to this moment, yet I'm doing it all again.

The battery never ran out. I'm never going to get old. I'm going to be doing this day forever.

December 24th Ver. 36

I can't cope with this anymore. I'm trapped in the house with this Christmas crazy idiot, and I can't do anything else. I dare not. What if I do something that causes him to die again? What happens then? I do the same day forever, but what happens afterwards. The rest of the world must go on after this day, but which one? What if it suddenly starts back up with my father dead? What if that's what it's waiting for? What if every day is another world, branching off into forever, can I keep him safe in all of them? Do I even want to anymore?

WHAT IF? WHAT IF? WHAT IF? WHAT IF? WHAT IF?

December 24th Ver. 86

Right, I think I've figured out a way to recalibrate the field from within it. I can alter the temporal array, and hopefully send myself forwards one day. I get to see tomorrow. After that, I simply alter it each day going forwards, and life might get to be almost normal. I can't escape the loop, but I can move it around the timeline…

December 24th T+1 year

The date isn't a mistake. I was being optimistic.
Turns out I can't move forward in units of 24 hours, I've
locked that in. I can only use the next level up - which is
years. So here I am, same spot as before, but exactly one year
later.

Dad is still alive, but in something of a state. As far as
he's concerned I disappeared a year ago, gone without a trace,
then suddenly I'm in my room on Christmas Eve.

I tried to explain, but it was a bit of a disaster. He's
pretty much convinced I'm a ghost. Perhaps I am.

December 24th T+1 year Ver. 2

I was better prepared this time. Dad woke this
morning to find a letter next to his bed, explaining about
Electrical Latency Fields, about time travel, about me. He
thought it was someone's idea of a sick joke, and started
searching the house for the perpetrator. He found me, sat at
the kitchen table, with a cooked breakfast and a mug of coffee
waiting for him.

We spent a lot of time talking. I'm not sure if he
believed me, or whether he thought he had gone mad. It
doesn't matter. I got to ask him the question.

"If you could choose, between never seeing me again,
or being trapped with me for eternity, what would you do?"

It was an unfair question, but I'm selfish, I had to ask.
If I'm honest I knew there was really only one answer he
would ever give. None the less, I had to hear it before I felt I
could do it.

December 24th Ver. 88

So I did it. I went back, and this time, I brought Dad into the field with me.

I had to explain everything again of course. He spent the first day lurching between confusion and sheer unadulterated joy. By today, he's just happy, particularly after discovering that our bank balance resets every time. He spent the afternoon trying to get as much money out of cash machines as possible.

I'm worried though, what if he can't deal with endless Christmas Eves? I had to get him just to keep myself sane, but who's going to look after him?

December 24th T+1 year Ver. 34

I've just read my last entry and laughed. Dad's amazing. He's having a whale of a time, and when it comes to exploring the possibilities of our situation, he's a genius of his own. By hopping back and forth between the original Christmas and this one we've learnt a lot about what the field lets you do. It's incredibly powerful. Whilst we're forced into a loop, our effects upon the outside world continue without us. If I leave a bundle of money under the floorboards, it's still there a year later.

It's better than that though. Say I leave the money under the floorboards, then flash back, take the money out of the bank again, and leave it in the coal cellar? When I go forwards in time, both piles of money are there. Any object can be replicated in this way, and continue to exist in multiple iterations of itself. Only things that are in some way sentient cannot. Any effect we have on people is a one off, but if we mess it up, we can always go back and have another go.

For the first time in our lives we're stupidly rich.

December 24th T+1 year Ver. 42

Dad's just thought to look up what happened to the reindeer. It turns out they disappeared at just the same time we did. I know what this means. So does Dad, he's spent the whole day grinning. We're going to have to go back, put the reindeer in the EL Field, and take them with us.

December 24th Ver. 109

I can't do it. It's impossible. I can't believe he asked me. He wants to go back in time and see Mum. It's not possible, and it should never be tried. Never.

December 24th Ver. 124

Dad says he believes in me. Says he knows I can do it. He keeps rustling my hair, and calling me his "little genius". I wrote him a list of all the reasons why it can't be done:

1)   We can't guarantee safe arrival. It's dangerous enough leaping into the future into a house that ought not to be occupied. Jumping back into a building that was owned by other people would be phenomenally dangerous, we might find ourselves merged with their bodies, or the furniture.
2)   The risk of paradox is massive. What if we accidentally wipe ourselves out?
3)   There is no way I can figure out a way to navigate the levels of quantum uncertainty that reversing the temporal field would induce.

He read it, scrunched it into a ball, shrugged, and said, "You'll crack it."

December 24th Ver. 136

I have a plan.

First Dad and I have to visit a friend.

December 24th T+20 years

The 34 year old Julie Finchley has a Nobel prize, a billion dollar technology company, a baby boy called William, and a husband called Gerald who paints watercolours for a living.

Meanwhile I haven't aged a day. I have my Dad and two reindeer.

I was right though. She is amazing. Yesterday we visited the 14 year old Julie with her parents. My Dad offered her an extremely large amount of sponsorship money, on two conditions. He explained that we had recently come into some money, and would be going away for a while. He asked that they ensure our house remained safe, intact and unoccupied, on Christmas Eve every year. They were welcome to do what they wanted with it the rest of the year.

Secondly the sponsorship would pay for Julie's education and research activities in perpetuity, so long as she dedicated a proportion of that time to solving a particularly difficult theoretical problem which had so far eluded me.

Today we went into the future to discover whether our investment had paid off. As hoped, Julie had done exactly as asked of her, and had spent considerable time and energy attempting to resolve the dilemma I presented to her that fateful evening. She was able to present a method that would, indeed, allow us to travel back in time, much to my father's delight.

She added that, according to her calculations, there was no way in which paradox could occur. That the universe was in a fixed state up to the moment of my creating the machine, but that such a state may well have included our prior existence. Whatever we do back then, we have already done. Finally, thanks to its mixed quantum state, the device would be utterly unable to deliver us to any place in which objects might already exist, or any region that was under direct observation.

Dad was glazing over at this point, so she simply reiterated that we could definitely go back. (Later she took me to one side and confessed that she had deduced our predicament, but had been unable to find any way to resolve it, much to her frustration. "Still, at least now you have a little more freedom within your prison.")

December 24th Ver. 144.

After all that fuss, Dad is putting it off. I don't understand adults.

December 24th Ver. 148

A thought occurred to me today. If we go back in time and meet Mum, wouldn't she have mentioned it? Wouldn't Dad know? I asked him about it, but he just got even more bad-tempered. "Don't you think I know that?" We had a massive row.

So that's it. We never go.

December 24th Ver. 149

We're going tomorrow! Dad apologised, said he wasn't sure if he was ready, but figured he never would be.

We did go. We do go. He's known it since the very first time I took him into the field and we looped back. He knew we could solve travelling back in time because he'd already met us in the past. He has told me about it, it's just at the time, neither of us knew it.

We go back in disguise. The day Mum and Dad met Santa.

December 24th T minus 14 years

I met my mother.

She was amazing. So beautiful, so smart, her eyes sparkled with life. She radiated warmth and love and… something. She was everything I had dreamt and imagined and so much more.

Before I saw her, I heard her. Dad had me hide round the side of their house and listen in at the window. She was arguing with him, my Dad back then, my Dad before me. They were arguing about Christmas. He, my Christmas obsessed Dad, was saying that the whole thing was stupid. A waste of time. That seeing as no family were coming over they should just forget the whole thing and have a few quiet days off.

She wasn't having any of it. You should have heard her. A time for magic and love, she said. "Magic and love". He laughed at her, said the whole thing was a big con, that it was just a way of making money, and an excuse to show bad telly for a couple of weeks. "Explain Father Christmas then," she said, resulting in the biggest laugh of all. My Dad could barely get his words out for incredulous guffaws, "There's…no…such…thing…"

At which point the doorbell rang, and my father managed to cross time and space just to prove himself wrong.

So we brought presents, and we cooked, and we talked, and we sang, and we played, and it was every bit as wonderful as my Dad had told me it was when he would whisper the story to me at Christmas Eve.

Leaving was hard. You could see Dad, watching the clock into the night. Suddenly he stood, "Well, must be off, presents to deliver." Santa Dad shook regular Dad by the hand, then kissed Mum ever so gently on the cheek. I ran over and hugged her. She was clearly a bit taken aback, but squeezed tightly all the same.

They lead us to the door, and as it closed behind us I allowed myself to study the pair of them one last time. Dad stood behind, his arms wrapped around my Mum and resting on the neat bulge in her abdomen that would soon give him a child, and rob him of a wife. She smiled softly, not knowing that this was the last Christmas she would enjoy. In those last seconds, she stared intently out at us, and called, "I think it's wonderful what you do. Wonderful." The door closed, and she was gone.

December 24th Ver. 150

I suggested to Dad that we go back and put Mum in the field with us. He refused, of course. "If she never has that baby, I never have you."

I suggested a return journey, but he refused that too. "That was it," he said, "that was what happened. Exactly what happened. We can never go again." Suddenly I understood why he had been so reluctant to visit her. "I got to say my goodbye. Besides she's told us what we need to do next."

I asked what he was talking about, but he just smiled mischievously.

December 24th Ver. 163

This morning Dad called me into the lounge, where he had laid out the Santa costume from his old job, and pointed at it with a grin. "We're ready."

I didn't get it. He opened the curtains and nodded to the reindeer meaningfully. They looked up briefly from chewing straw, and seemed amused by my confusion.

Dad rolled his eyes. "We have infinite money and resources. We can fly anywhere in the world, at any time in history, as many times as we like, so long as its Christmas Eve."

He threw his arms wide in expectation, still nothing.

"Oh come on, you even called your time travel field thingy the ELF, what more do you need?"

I finally understood.

"Come on son, it's what she would have wanted."

He's right, it is. It really is.

December 24th Ver. 9546

It's wonderful what we do. Wonderful!

Dad and I get to spend the rest of eternity ensuring that for one night every year, the world is bathed in "magic and love."

It was a bit chaotic at first, but now we're getting good at it. We make millions of journeys, all in one evening, looping time over and over again. We copy thousands of toys, storing them safely out of the way at the North Pole before delivering them to children everywhere, the E.L.F. depositing us whilst they sleep.

All in the memory of one woman who felt that Christmas is, was, and always should be, special.

My Dad is so amazing.

My Dad is Father Christmas.

About the Authors

Richard Mark Bacon BSc (Hons)
Richard Bacon was born in Nottingham, England, where he still resides with his wife and daughter.
Richard has had a keen interest in books and reading since an early age, as well as a highly active imagination. Now a 'grown up' he has begun writing down his ideas and is now almost constantly working on, or thinking about, new ideas and adventures.

Beth Bowler
Beth Bowler is a graduate of the University of Wolverhampton School of Arts and Design. Since graduating Beth has been working as a primary school teacher. She has also been developing her skills as a creative writer, a hobby that has been burning in the background of her career. However creative writing occasionally takes lead priority as it likes to remind her of its importance in her life. Beth sees her creativity as a separate life force, symbiotically coexisting within her and demanding a right to exist. Fortunately she is driven by this along with the desire to use story telling as a tool for communicating important messages, bringing them to life in the hearts and minds of children young and old. Last year Beth won her first writing competition, and is now pleased to be a part of this collection, presenting to you 'The Princess and the Gardener'.

J.R. Troughton
James Ross Troughton grew up in a very small village next to a very big road in Cambridgeshire. Now he resides in Seoul, living with his girlfriend and a small kitten, earning his keep by teaching small children how to speak English and how to add numbers. Occasionally he teaches them not to bite each other.

Chris Preece

Chris Preece lives in Yorkshire with his wife, 2 children and a spider called Sidney. (Who may or may not be more than one spider, but as long as he's called Sidney, no-one seems to mind.)

In between healing the sick, and catering to the whims of children, he sometimes finds time to piece together whole sentences for his own amusement.

Chris Lill

Chris Lill wishes the world was free from suffering and pain, Nissan Micras, Mushrooms, reality TV, low slung jeans and all use of the word 'izzit'. When he's not failing to live up to his potential he pontificates, tuts, casts aspersions and revels in pedantry. Overall, he's remarkably unremarkable apart from his unrelenting desire to prove that sarcasm is much more than the lowest form of wit.

Andrew Merson

Andrew Merson started writing 'what I did on holiday' at school, moved on to angst-ridden teenage poetry for disinterested girls, and progressed to music reviews for the university newspaper. He was a regular script contributor to the Aberdeen Students Charities Campaign Student Show. He lives in Aberdeenshire, works as a Police Officer, and writes nonsense that nobody is supposed to see.

Paul Tonner

Paul Tonner is an Illustrator and all round design bloke from Brigadoon in Scotland. He is 'all round' because he loves the cheese toasties a little too much. He has done quite a lot of album covers and doodles over the last few years. One day he might even make some money from doing it. His favourite colour is cat and his favourite animal is purple.

10200453R00057

Made in the USA
Charleston, SC
15 November 2011